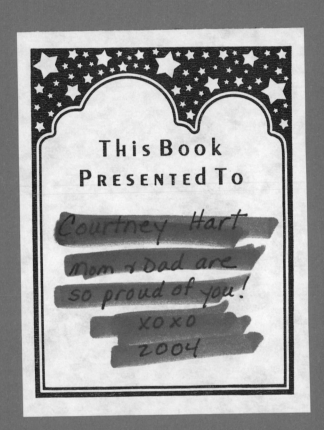

This Book
PRESENTED To

Courtney Hart
mom + Dad are
so proud of you!
XOXO
2004

I Know It's Autumn

By Eileen Spinelli
Illustrated by Nancy Hayashi

HARPERCOLLINSPUBLISHERS

I Know It's Autumn
Text copyright © 2004 by Eileen Spinelli Illustrations copyright © 2004 by Nancy Hayashi
Manufactured in China by South China Printing Company Ltd. All rights reserved.
www.harperchildrens.com

Library of Congress Cataloging-in-Publication Data
Spinelli, Eileen.
　I know it's autumn / by Eileen Spinelli ; illustrated by Nancy Hayashi.— 1st ed.
　　p.　cm.
　Summary: A rhyming celebration of the sights, smells, and sounds of autumn, such as pumpkin muffins, turkey
stickers on spelling papers, and piles of raked leaves.
　ISBN 0-06-029422-1— ISBN 0-06-029423-X (lib. bdg.)
　[1. Autumn—Fiction. 2. Stories in rhyme.] I. Hayashi, Nancy, ill. II. Title.
PZ8.3.S759Iae 2004　　　　　　　　　　　　　　　　　　　　　　　　　　　　　　　2003004099
[E]—dc21

Typography by Matt Adamec
1 2 3 4 5 6 7 8 9 10
❖
First Edition

For Sharon and Sam
Addie and Jack
Pat and Jim
—E.S.

To David and Brian
—N.H.

I know it's autumn when
the morning light comes late,

when there's a pumpkin muffin
on my breakfast plate.

When Daddy brings my jacket
from the storage box,

and Grandpop wears a bathrobe
and his slipper socks.

I know it's autumn when
the school bus toots its horn,
when we drive past an empty field
that once grew corn.

When leafy trees turn colors—
red, gold and brown—

and Farmer Freddy brings
his harvest into town.

I know it's autumn when
our class makes acorn art,

when there's a turkey sticker
on each spelling chart,

when we help Mrs. Martin
bake zucchini bread

and yellow mums are blooming
in the flower bed.

I know it's autumn when
we rake the leaves in piles,
when doorstep jack-o'-lanterns
wear their crooked smiles,

when we go picking apples
for Mom's apple pie,

and noisy geese fly south
across the evening sky.

I know it's autumn when
the moon is full and bright,
when we go on a hayride
with our friends at night.

When bonfires blaze and the storyteller
leaps and claps,

and all the kids grow sleepy
on their daddies' laps.

Sweet autumn dreams, everyone!